The Aaron Sans Erotica Collection
Volume 7

Anal Sex and Butt Stuff

Aaron Sans

Contents

Romp on the Beach: Sex and Anal Play with a Stranger off the Internet

Mark picked me up at midnight. For hours I have been trying to stop the butterflies from dancing in my stomach. We met the night before. He was the first of my online dating experiences. I was nervous and excited. I ran out the door, and jumped into his green SUV. He reeked of confidence and sexuality. His arms were muscular and heavily tattooed. We drove around to the North Shore of Oahu, and made small talk about how amazing it was that we hit it off so quickly. I wasn't sure what was going to happen, but the anticipation was driving me up the wall. He picked a very quiet beach. Remote with no houses in sight, and pulled over. He reached across the seat, and kissed me. His lips touched mine, and immediately sent fire through my belly. I could feel my pussy getting wet. I wanted him. I could only hope at this point he wanted me back.

We walked hand in hand down to the beach. He had conveniently packed a large blanket. After spreading it out, we sat down close to each other. The beach was perfect tonight. The moon was bright, and the waves were so loudly crashing down around us. I was nervous, and just gazing out into the water, afraid to look him in the eyes.

We talked about everything. Kids, Marriage, Love. He told me how beautiful I was. He could not understand why I was single. Why I was online dating.

Finally I gathered enough courage to kiss him again. I pushed him down on the blanket, and sat on top of him. My wet pussy was pressed against his jeans. I aggressively kissed him. Sucking on his tongue and lips. His hands were roaming all over my body. With every touch, he was driving my body more and more insane. He rolled me over, and allowed his body to hoover over mine. He had his knee in between my legs. He kissed my neck and my ears, so sweetly. He pulled my dress down to my waist. Mark started to caress my breast through my bra while continuing to kiss my lips. He pulled my bra straps down one at a time. He very gently placed his hands on the clasp behind my back. He looked at my eyes, and I knew that he was silently asking me if what he was doing was okay. I just nodded my head. I did not want to say anything in fear of ruining the moment. With one move of his skilled hand, my bra was laying on the blanket. I was now almost naked on the beach, while Mark was still fully dressed.

He took one of my nipples into his mouth. My entire body had become an electrical current. He sucked gently and expertly. His hand was massaging my other nipple. They were so hard. He was switching back and forth to give both of my nipples the attention they needed. The breeze was perfectly hitting the wetness. I wanted Mark, and he knew it. I could feel the moisture coming down inside of my pussy. My panties were now evidently wet. With his mouth on my nipple, he took his hand and placed them inside of my panties. I moaned, for it had been years since I have been touched this way.

I wanted him to make me cum. I needed an orgasm. Mark dipped his index finger into my wetness. He very slowly and perfectly started rubbing my clit. He would wait until I was almost to climax, and stop to dip his finger into my pussy again. I did not know how much more I could take. I needed my control back. As much as I wanted to cum, I knew that once I did, Mark had me, I would belong to him.

I removed his hand, and rolled over on top of him. I placed his hands behind his back. I began unbuckling his belt with my teeth. I had never done this before, and I realized that it is quite easy. I unbuttoned his pants, slowly. I wanted him to want me as badly as I wanted him. I pulled his pants down to his knees. To my pleasant surprise he wasn't wearing any underwear. I sat back and just took in the sight of his amazing cock. It was one of the nicest ones I have ever seen. I couldn't wait to get that in my mouth.

I immediately stuck his dick in my mouth. I wanted it to touch the back of my throat. My goal was to touch his balls with my tongue and gag on his dick at the same time. What a lovely fucking dick he had. I started bobbing my head and at the same time grasping him firmly at the base of his cock. My split was all over him. Sucking his dick turned me on more than Mark touching me would ever do. I knew he was close to cumming, and I wanted to swallow every drop of his juice.

Abruptly, he stopped me. He rolled me over, and got behind me. Mark ripped my panties and he struggled to get them off. He took my arms and pulled them behind my back, holding them with one strong hand, and had my hair wrapped tightly around his other fist. The first moment of penetration was crazy. I wanted to explode all around him. He was slamming inside of me. It was so hard, so fast, and so fucking amazing. His balls were slapping my already sensitive clit. He let go of my arms, and placed my hands in front on me on my clit. I had no clue what was coming next.

He pulled out of my pussy, and pushed my head down into the blanket. My pussy felt empty and my ass was in the air. He started tonguing my ass. Jamming his tongue in and out, and at the same time fingering my pussy. I was going to cum. I couldn't stop it this time. My body started tensing up and I started shaking. I let myself release. I started moaning and squirming. Mark replaced his tongue with his thumb. He very slowing starting working it in and out of my ass.

All of the sudden he jammed his dick back inside of my pussy. I knew that he wouldn't last much longer. He kept pumping away. I was going to cum again. I couldn't stop shaking. I felt full. His dick in my pussy and thumb in my ass was exactly what I needed. Mark pulled his dick out and flipped me over. He sprayed my face with warm salty semen. I stuck my tongue out hoping to get a taste of him.

After he was done, he started licking his own cum off of my face. He would rotate from licking my face, to kissing me. I had never before that moment tasted a man's cum from his own tongue.

After he had me cleaned up, he helped me put my bra back on, and pulled my dress back up. We folded up the blanket and started walking back to the car. There was nothing but silence. I didn't know what to say. That was one of the best, and most erotic sexual experiences I had ever had.

As we pulled away from the beach, my only thoughts were about how many other men there were on that dating site. With this as my first date, I can only imagine how much sex I was going to have. I waited years for this experience, and it was amazing, but I couldn't wait to get back home, and answer another man's email. I have a feeling, my pussy will never be lonely again.

All Holes With The Fuck Buddy

"I would much rather have your sister," bare-chested Keith whispered in her ear.

"Well, she doesn't want you, so you better settle for…." Before she could finish the sentence, he had flung her on his bed. He did not even kiss her. He immediately started to grope her. He ran his fingers between her legs. Through her pants, he could feel her wet, hot, eager pussy. Her leg quivered, she wanted nothing more than for him to fuck her, and the harder he would do it the better! No man had fucked her in over two years, so there was no way in hell that she would go for two more years without the touch of a man!

Keith was all that she needed; her main desire, at the moment. Oh yes, she wanted to come over and over on his dick.

"Aw…" she moaned.

"You want it, don't you! You really want this dick!"

"Fuck, yes, and it's about time that you give it to me!"

"Not just yet, Susan, if you want it in your pussy you have to get it in the other two holes first!"

"You drive a hard bargain, but sure, whatever you want." She moved gently from underneath him to take an upmost position. She took off his pants and his boxers, "You won't need these, Keith."

He smiled, "Will you….Oh…yes baby…That is so fucking good!" Her lips hugged his dick like a sloth on the branches of a tree. "Yes, honey, suck me dry!"

"That's just what I intend to do, baby!" Damn, his dick was so warm and delicious like freshly baked pastry. She could suck him forever. Ten minutes later, he decided to take charge. Instead of laying her on the bed, he bent her over on her knees. Unbuttoned her pants, took them off, removed and sniffed her panties. Patting her on the ass, he said, "Now, you are gonna get it!"

He tore her blouse off of her luscious skin. He stroked her breast and pressed his dick firmly against her butt cheek. "Are you ready?"

"Yes, Keithy baby." He pushed the entirety of his dick directly into her ass. "Fuck! This shit hurts, but I kinda like it."

"Of course you do!"

"Gosh, you are so fucking huge! I love a big dick; it's my favorite kind."

"I'm a size 11 baby! So enjoy!" He fucked her so long and so hard, she felt like she was about to pass out, but she was enjoying it.

"Ok, that's enough. Now, I will give you what I promised you, right after I eat up that pussy of yours!" She laid on the bed and opened her legs. "You have a beautiful pussy."

She chuckled, "To think that you would have preferred my sister's."

He smirked, "I still want to fuck her, but will fuck you first" He started to play with her pussy. He rubbed her clit with one finger, then two. She was really wet. He shoved both fingers inside of her warm crabby. Her legs trembled from all the excitement. He stroked her pussy. "I'm really going to enjoy fucking you," he said. He, then, dove down right in the middle of her beautiful pink vagina. He started to eat that pussy like it was nobody else's business. She moaned and groaned. He pushed his tongue inside her pussy and started to tongue-fuck her.

Fuck this man can eat, she thought to herself. A few minutes later, she felt it. She knew it. She was about to explode. She could not help it! Hot goo burst out of her cunny hole, right in his mouth and down his throat.

"Ok, that's it! I've made you cum. Now, it's my turn." She felt his warm dick as it pressed against her inner thigh as he prepared it for its destination.

"Are you sure that your small hole can handle this entire dick!"

"Well, if my ass could handle it, there is no reason that my cunny can't. Besides, I want you. All of you, and…Fuck!"

"What? Is it too much? Thought you could handle it!" He proceeded to fuck her. It did hurt her like hell at first, but afterwards; she had no problem accepting the full cock! They were both hot, wet and dripping with sweat. He raised her legs above his shoulder for better penetration. Gosh, she loved every inch of him. Now, he was a really good fuck buddy. He really knew how to make her pussy water. In fact, she came over and over on his fat, long dick. Each time she came, he felt more inspired; he intensified the fucking.

"I want it doggy style!" she exclaimed. "I want to feel your entire depth in my pussy, and I want you to fuck me as hard as you can!" She positioned on the bed for him. He rubbed his fingers over her pussy from behind to test her level of wetness.

"Are you sure that this is what you want?

"Yes, please. Give me, everything."

"Okay, at your request." With one great push, the entire 11inches went in.

She screamed bloody hell from pain and delight. He bumped and grind her cunny. Her liquid combined with his sweat flowed down her legs. His balls were all wet, dripping with her pour. They fucked for two hours and then, he grabbed hold of his dick, squeezed it very tightly to prevent his precious contents from spilling. He lowered her on the pillow and he shoved his thickness in her mouth, "Suck it; I want to feel my dick touch the back of your throat."

She complied. She gave him a deep throated suck. As he exploded into her mouth, she could feel his sticky wet warmness going down her throat. She savored his taste. They both laid in bed tired from all the excitement of the day. He played with her breasts, and looked at her, "Today was fun. Maybe we can fuck again sometime soon." She smiled in agreement.

"Next time, Susan, bring your sister along with you!"

Anal Pleasures with a Demon Whore from a Costume Party: An Erotic Story with Snowballing

He woke up to the sound of his alarm clock buzzing around on his side table. He reached over without a thought and slapped the "snooze" button and rolled back on his side. It was a Friday, and he was going to a party later that night with a few of the guys from work. The alarm clock started its dreadful buzzing again and fell off the table. Annoyed, James finally got out of his bed and walked to the bathroom to shave and clean up. Before leaving the bathroom to get dressed, he looked in the mirror and decided to keep his bed-head hairdo and smiled and winked at himself. He shut off the light, marched into his room, and grabbed his white dress shirt with his crimson tie and threw on his beige slacks. He sighed a relief as he marked today's date with a red "X" and chugged out of the gallon of orange juice. Then he grabbed his keys and started out the door to his boring office job.

James couldn't get something off his mind while he was on his daily commute to work. The thought that today was going to be different. He felt that the day was going faster than usual. There was barely any traffic, and he was excited to go to the party later that night with Will and Frankie from work. It was a costume party, and he already planned on being a firefighter. Will was dressing up as a Cop, and Frankie would be Abraham Lincoln.

As soon as the clock on his computer hit 4:30, He saved his document and ran out the door to his car and sped home. As soon as he got home, he kicked off his shoes and tossed his keys on the table. He raced up his stairs to his closet and took off all his clothes and jumped in the shower and started washing his hair and chest, then slowly went down to his dick. He knew he would be around women tonight and has the chance to get some, so he starts scrubbing his dick. He always enjoyed washing his dick. He would always put extra shampoo on his hands and would start jacking off. It was his favorite guilty pleasure. He would always think about Christina, the receptionist from work who always wears those sexy V-necks with her double D breasts practically hanging out of her shirt. He moaned softly and started jerking off faster and imagined her sucking his dick while it's between her big and voluptuous breasts. And then right before he blew his load in her mouth, she pulled it out and made him cum all over her cute little face. He came all over his hands and let out a soft and long moan.

He washed himself off as fast as he possibly could and got out to put on his costume. He rushed as he pulled on his yellow fireman jacket over his white t-shirt and kept it unbuttoned while he pulled on his suspenders and grabbed his hat. He was out the door to the party.

He pulled up to the party and saw Will and Frankie waiting outside. He ran over to them and they all walked inside together. There were people everywhere, tons. People he never met before, but there was a girl, dressed up like some kind of demon-whore. She was gorgeous, and she saw him too. He couldn't take his eyes off her. About an hour passed, and he finally built up the courage to walk up to her and ask her name.

"Hey" James said, "I couldn't help but stare. I hope I didn't offend you."

The demon-whore lady chuckled. "It's alright! I usually don't like be stared at by creeps, but you can watch me for as long as you want. I'm Maia."

James smiled, then replied "I'm James. What kind of name is Maia?"

"Beats me!" Maia said. "You could ask my parents, but I don't think my folks would like you."

James opened his mouth to talk but realized it would get drowned out by the loud music that was playing. He smiled and grabbed her by the hand and pulled her outside of the building. Maia followed willingly and stopped as soon as they got outside and pulled him to her and kissed him. James pulled back in shock and stared at her seductive smile, grabbed her firm ass, looked at her curiously. She closed her eyes and bit her lip softly when he touched her ass. When he stopped she looked at him and smiled.

"Take me somewhere... private," she said as seductive as she possibly could. James couldn't help but run to his car and open the door for her. She stepped in and smiled at his generosity, and he shut the door behind her. He jumped in the driver's seat and drove her home. All the way home, she had her hand on his thigh rubbing his dick as he drove. When they got to his house, he picked her up over his shoulder and brought her to his room. He threw her on the bed and started kissing her while he pulled down his pants. Her costume was very thin and she clearly had nothing on under it. He started slowly reaching for her breasts, and she grabbed him and threw him on the bed. She laughed at him, and grabbed his tie from the clothes he wore to work that morning. She looked down at him and grabbed his hands and put them together and tied them with his tie.

James willingly let her tie him up because it was something he always wanted to do. She looked down at him and rubbed his dick through his underwear. All she could think about is how hard and big it was and how it would fit in her tight asshole. "I'm your master now, and you'll treat me as such." She proclaimed. "Understand?"

He looked up at her, this beautiful woman he hadn't even known for more than about 2 hours had him tied up and all he could say was "Yes, Master Maia."

"Good." She straddled him and started rubbing the crotch of her costume against his hard dick in its cloth confinement. She loved it. She grabbed both his hands and started to suck on his fingers as if she was sucking on his hard delicious dick. Her pussy was getting wet. Fast. She pulled him off the bed and on to his knees and stood in-front of him.

"Take off my panties" She ordered "with your teeth." James looked up at her shyly, then leaned in slowly, and bit her panties and pulled them down to her ankles. She lifted her feet out of them. She pulled them from James' mouth and smacked him across the face with them. She pushed his head back against the bed and sat on his mouth. Making sure her wet pussy was on his lips, and before she could tell her new little toy to start eating her out, she could feel his tongue inside her... his long, thick, and wet tongue just wiggling around inside her. She couldn't help but let out a loud squeal. James noticed and kept licking her, trying to explore her and find her "G-spot." She noticed he liked her juices and teasingly stood up all the way and spread her ass cheeks.

All she could feel was his tongue against her asshole and she loved it. She fell to her knees and put her ass in the air to let him keep licking her. He took this as a chance to make her his toy now. He broke free of the tie and teasingly forced his tongue into her asshole, his cock just stood straight up. He pulled his tongue back into his mouth and spanked her tight, firm ass. He took his long and hard dick, meanwhile she starts to look back confused, and he starts to smack his dick against her asshole. Maia lets out a small moan. "Please stop beating around the bush and pound me," she begged.

James bit his lip and pushed the head of his dick against her ass and tried to force it in, but it was too tight so he decided to start fucking her tight and dripping pussy. He started slow, forcing his entire dick inside her as she moaned softly when he her skin touched his balls. Then slowly pulled the entire dick out and then slowly, but progressively, faster. Maia was moaning, begging for more, with her face against the floor. James forced his finger into her tight ass and started fingering her. Maia started moaning louder and panting faster, and saying she's going to cum. James pulled out and flipped her on her back. He began to smack her pussy softly watching her facial expression hoping she will cum for him.

"Mmmm... James, I want you to eat my cum right out of me," Maia proclaimed. James willingly starts licking her pussy and fingering her asshole again, hoping to loosen it up. She wiggled around and let out a loud squeal and came on his mouth. He smiled as she let out a loud sigh of relief and laid back as James cleans up all of her delicious cum. She starts to get up and crawl on the bed, meanwhile James forced his dick into her asshole.

"You thought we were done? You must not know me all that well" James said as he started pounding her tight asshole as hard as he could. Maia let out the loudest moan she made all night and started fucking him as hard as she could. She loved his large and hard dick in her tight ass. She didn't even care if he came inside her. She wanted his cum. She wanted him. James noticed her increased enthusiasm and let her take control while he tried to hold his cum in. She started moaning louder and fucked him harder, making sure his dick went as deep as possible. James couldn't hold in his moans and began to start moaning her name louder. She heard him and it made her want him more. She started pounding him harder and harder. James couldn't handle it and moaned as he filled her ass with his cum. He got on his knees and started sucking on her asshole and sucking his cum out. Once he got a mouthful, he started kissing her, moving it all to her mouth. They made out back and forth like this for about 10 minutes before she swallowed it.

Another Man for My Wife's Birthday: Anal Threesome Fun

We had been together 10 years, so when it came time for my wife's birthday that particular year, I was kind of stumped on what she wanted that I hadn't already got her. All the times she used to ride me until I came inside her, I found myself frequently whispering to her if she would be turned on with another hard dick to hold on to while she fucked me. Seeing her become excited when we were out and another prick entertained her dirty thoughts, and with how much she loved sucking cock, sometimes it turned me on thinking about her fantasies coming to life.

When her 30th birthday was coming around I asked her what she wanted, and she giggled confessing to me she really wanted to bring a partner in the bedroom… another man, and to suck and fuck him while I watched. I obliged, and on the night of her birthday we responded to an ad on a local web site after some searching for the right candidates. She picked him out, a semi muscular man with a thick rock hard cock, its throbbing head curved upwards. Several pictures of his cock accompanied his profile, and she became very excited. After exchanging emails, he was on his way, and the fantasy was taking shape.

Slipping into a silk button up dress shirt and silk tight pants, she answered the door for him, pulling the stud inside and demanding he take a seat before sticking her tits in his face, grinding her wet pussy through her pants on his cock. He grasped her tits through the smooth silk, soaking it with spit as he gently took playful bites at her rock solid nipples. I couldn't take it. When I got up to sit next to them she pushed me down, "You're going to look, NOT fucking touch" she snarled.

I sat back down hurriedly, not before she took leather restraints and locked my hands to the chair. She told him to get up, and pulled his big dick out to start licking it, pulling it straight up and slowly teasing it with her tongue from his balls to his tip, his knees shuddering in pleasure. "This is how you suck cock," she said, "you feel the tip in my mouth and my tongue. I want to taste cum," she told him.

"How does his hard dick taste?" she asked me, using her tongue to lick the inside of my mouth before pulling my head back and slowly letting her spit run into my mouth. Pulsing my hips into the air she could tell I was yearning for her to taste my shaft, and she pulled it out, excitedly giving both of us head. Making him sit on my lap naked, stroking his needy cock, she got underneath him and cleaned his asshole, sucking his balls and pleasing his ass while he stroked his shaft.

"Fuck my ass," she told him as he stood up and picked her small frame into the air, holding her completely up, his dick disappearing up her ass. Grinding her ass up him against roughly, it's how she always liked it, her asshole taken when you fucked. Rubbing her slit now facing me while he rode her from behind, she held my shoulders as I was seated while he tried his best not to cum.

"I'm fucking cumming!" she yelled. "Don't you fucking stop!" Her cunt began squirting cum all over my legs as she squeezed her tits and glared at me with a nasty grin, laughing.

"Is this what you needed baby? Is this what you wanted for your present?" I asked.

"Oh fuck yes! I'm your filthy fucking whore; fill my fucking asshole full of cum," she told him as he grunted and groaned, squirts of his hot cum no doubt slipping out in her, until he threw his head back and exploded inside her ass, filling it up with cum.

"Good boy," she told him, the pleasure on both their faces as she slowly still worked up and down, back and forth gyrating on his dick. She wasn't done... no not even close. Leading him into the bedroom, she fit him into a latex bodysuit and mask, the only exposed part of his body was his long curved prick. She lay him on his back on the bed, and sank her pussy down on him, riding his dick even harder, cum leaking from her fucked asshole slowly drizzled out on the latex suit. Now unhooked, I stood in front of her stroking my dick, twisting my hand around the head needing to cum so bad. I couldn't get it out fast enough. I couldn't decide if i wanted to fuck her or jerk off as hard and fast as I could with her urging me to cum in her mouth.

Pulling her hair back, I jacked myself off, spraying hot cum up her chest and into her mouth, in her excitement she came again, squirting cum all over the latex suit he was in. She pulled his dick out of her, soaking wet with cum everywhere and sucked him until he shot a 2nd load into the air. She giggled and unzipped his mask, covered in cum rubbing herself all over him. It was so fucking hot after a few minutes I couldn't take it, and came from behind entering her tight ass.

"Ohhhh fuck yes," she threw he head back, succumbing to another shaft filling her ass. "Fuck my ass until you cum you dirty fucker," she taunted me, sprawled out on top of his cum covered suit. His flaccid dick hanging there, all cummed out, as he continued holding her hips steady so I could fill her up. I felt another load coming so hard it hurt, the first squirt I let go into her ass, then I pulled out and quickly shot the rest in her needy pussy hole, shrieking in ecstasy.

"Was that the best birthday ever?" I asked her after we escorted the man out.

"Yes, baby," she replied, "how will you top this next year?"

Threesome with Two Women: DP with a Strap-On

I got into the hobby with a goal in mind; to have my first duo. I didn't want just any duo though, so I began "auditions" if you will, to find the perfect girls for me. Ashley has a sexy petite body and a knack for detail and knowing what you need. Lily has a killer body and an appetite for sex while looking deceivingly demure.

I first met Ashley back in August, and she immediately became the focus of all my thoughts. Her attention to detail is what sets her apart from the rest. Then I met Lily in September, and I knew they would fit perfectly together even though they had never met.

So in the months that followed several attempts were made to get the two of them together, but our schedules never quite lined up. Finally everything lined up last month and it was everything I'd hoped it would be and then some.

Ashley is a world traveler, each meeting is an investment in time and the dividends are her undivided attention to your every desire. Based on other times I've seen her, I believe she has the ability to become anyone you want her to be, and she pulls off the slutty rocker chic look and personality that I love so well. Ok, enough preamble.

Setting up with Lily & Ashley was actually pretty easy, I booked a room for us to play in so once we all committed to a date and time I knew I could count on them. They are both very communicative in the time leading up to the date so you are never left in the dark.

I met Ashley at the hotel bar at the set time and Lily was scheduled to arrive a half hour later. Being that it was Thursday afternoon, the bar was almost empty. Ashley greeted me as always, with a sexy smile, bright eyes and a very sensual long kiss. She has the softest tongue but isn't shy about using it. She was dressed in mostly black as I like and even remembered to wear a cute pink collar that I had jokingly mentioned the last time we met. Since we were waiting on Lily, we ordered some drinks. We both got Jack & Coke, she took some in her mouth and let me suck it out as we sat there and she swayed to the rock music I had playing on the jukebox.

We moved to a dark corner of the bar and I pulled her top down to play with her perky pink nipples. After some more swapping Jack, she got under the table and gave me a very aggressive but quick blowjob, let me tell you, this girl has absolutely no gag reflex. In a previous meeting I face-fucked her pretty hard and came straight down her throat, she never gagged, I was in heaven. A text from Lily and a few minutes later we all went to the room.

Ashley let her in as I followed, I had a raging hard on in anticipation of the events about to unfold. They introduced themselves and shared a sexy kiss before coming to me. We had a short 3-way kiss, Lily quickly got naked and Ashley and I commented about her beautiful Venus De Milo type body. Soon they were both on their knees sharing my cock. Both are aggressive deep throaters and they took turns.

They followed my every direction, both swirling their tongues around the head of my cock as if they were making love to it with their mouths. I was already on visual and sensory over load at this point, so we took a break to all get naked and in bed. Something I had heard about in college, champagne waterfalls, sounds fun, but in practice it's awkward and messy, but still fun. I had Lily sit over my face as Ashley dribbled Jack & Coke down Lily's body from her chest into my mouth, problem was just as much got into my eyes so we quickly abandoned that idea. The next several hours were a blur.

I made sure to check off the few things I wanted to do, Lily riding my face and Ashley riding my cock while they both made out. I heard Ashley ask her if my tongue was in her ass, she said yea, then Ashley came around and said 'does her ass taste good?' then sucked my tongue. Damn I love that dirty girl.

Ashley brought some various dildos, she doesn't do anal but Lily loves it, so I thought some double penetration was in order. Lily got on top of me in reverse cowgirl and Ashley slowly guided my cock into Lily's creamy white ass while Ashley was playing with her strap on and entered her pussy. Several times I could feel what Ashley was doing inside Lily on my cock, incredible!

Lily laid back on me and started saying 'Im gonna cum', I squeezed her tits tight as Ashley and I worked her over front and back until she was a hot sweaty mess laying on top of me. We took a short breather, had some more Jack swapping, now it was time for the finale, double throat job with them sharing my cum. We worked up to it, one doing deep throat while sloppily kissing the other and them switching places. I was way over stimulated, so I really had to focus to get off. I think Ashley sensed that and started with some hot dirty talk to get me there. When I finally got close, Ashley joined her between my legs and they both went porn star crazy sharing my cum, tongues and cum sliding all over their faces.

The time of my life. We slept a little while in a sticky pile, Lily had other obligations so she got dressed and left, but Ashley and I enjoyed winding down together. She cleaned me up but we left that room a mess.

My Best Friend's MILF and Our Smoking Fetish, Anal Sex, and Squirting

Sandy was so sexy. And my best friend's mother, twenty-some years my senior. Always flirting with her son's friends, trying to get a rise out of us. About 5'6" 100 lbs, Sandy had a sexy deep smoker's voice and perky tits she wasn't afraid to go braless with. On more than one occasion I recall her sitting on my lap at their house, leaning in asking me to light her 120 cigarettes. She was so fucking sexy smoking, always taking long deliberate drags. Sandy enjoyed every cigarette she smoked, often switching brands and talking about how she enjoyed the flavors. Sometimes I would have to almost rush home or into their bathroom and jerk off right then, wishing I was lighting her cigarette for her to suck my needy cock off while exhaling smoke all over me.

Some years later I ran into Sandy at the mall, being the very touchy affectionate type when I said hello she gave me a big hug. Her jeans were so tight they hugged her ass perfectly, her tits slightly protruding from the sleeveless button up shirt she had on. She had no idea I had been jerking off to her for years, wishing I could cum inside her. Her smell was incredible when she hugged me, that of perfume masking the cigarette smell. I made sure she saw me look her top to bottom, several times, and I expressed to her I hadn't seen her son in a few years… I would love to have lunch and catch up. We chatted for a few more minutes, and then hugged again, this time she gave me a kiss on the cheek, which I returned just as quick, getting rather close to her mouth.

A week later, Sandy called. She said she was running some errands if I wanted to meet that afternoon for lunch, which I excitedly agreed too. I was so fucking horny heading to meet her, not really expecting much just proud of the fact this was happening. Lunch went good, and some flirting ensued. As we were leaving the restaurant, as soon as we exited, she immediately put a cigarette to her mouth. "I'll light that," I insisted. holding the lighter slightly back so she had to come to it. We each had a few drinks, and she could tell I was enjoying her lighting up. Then she said it. Asked me if I enjoyed watching her smoke. Like an over excited puppy, I said that I loved it. It was my fantasy to light her cigarettes. Surprised, she laughed and said I could light all her cigarettes, now turning so her ass pressed against my pulsating rock hard cock. I pushed gently up against her, feeling as if I could cum right then.

"I will call you" she said as she exhaled and flicked her cigarette, giving me one last long hug before she left. Thankfully Sandy wasted no time, and the next night we were on our way a bar. We had to go quite a distance away so she didn't have to worry about her husband or being seen by any family. We joked and flirted the whole way. Several times she would reach over and rub the inside of my legs, coming close to the head of my dick. The night pressed on, into the wee morning hours, and Sandy decided we should get a hotel. She had been dancing and grinding on me all night, every head in the bar watching us more than likely thinking she was my mother when we first arrived.

Inside the hotel room she pushed me on the bed, opening my pants up revealing my swollen cock. She took her leather cigarette case, rubbing it up and down the shaft of my prick, meanwhile kissing up the insides of my legs. Before I knew it she was stroking me and licking my asshole. I had never had that done, at first I squirmed then I started working my ass hole into her tongue, moving my hips up and down as she tugged my cock.

"Is this my cock now?" she asked kissing my balls. I confessed to her how I had jerked off so many times to her... how I had jerked off in her panties in their bathroom, just the smell of her sweet pussy made me cum. I had to taste her pussy, every piece of her. I licked her freckled skin from shoulders down to her slightly hairy crotch. Mounting my face, Sandy ground her clit on my mouth as I used my hands to feel every inch of her body, unsure if this would be my only chance to fuck her. She rode my tongue faster, threatening me that she was going to cum, until she went from my mouth to my prick that was standing up. She immediately came all over me, sitting down to my balls squirting a stream of cum up to my belly button. I held her tiny ass in one hand, pulling her hair with the other as we stared in each other's eyes, almost angrily fucking. I had to pull my cock out to cum. I couldn't take it and exploded all over her, only for Sandy to push my dick back in her before I was done cumming. I grunted in pleasure feeling the last few pumps of my jizz fill her.

"I want it fucking rough, give me that young cock! It's mine now," Sandy whispered to me as I flipped her doggy style taking my belt and putting it around her hips. Using the belt I thrust her hips into me, using my fingers to open her tight asshole and massage it, spitting on her ass crack telling her she better cum again for daddy. She loved it, proceeding to cum again. This time I got my face down there helping her squirt while she was on all fours. I sank my prick back in her, telling her I wasn't done… that I was going to fill her with cum. She begged for me to unload in her ass, so I rode her as hard as I could, in pure ecstasy awaiting another thick load. Feeling my cock working itself full of cum, Sandy leaned her head back for me to light her cigarette while I fucked her. Her tight body and long cigarette drags forced me too cum, letting my cock glide between her ass crack until it pumped another hot cum load on her. Sandy wiggled her ass around on me as I shuddered in disbelief how incredible that was.

"Does this mean from now on this is my cock?" she said exhaling smoke. I furiously kissed her, telling her I was hers anytime.

My Girlfriend's Anal Virginity

One winter I was at home enjoying my whiskey and watching a movie when I received a call from my girlfriend at around midnight. I could tell by her voice that she was feeling nasty as she told me that she wanted to see me immediately. I told her I'd be there within the hour

I finished my drink as my mind began running. She was living with her parents and an older sister, and it was one in the morning almost by the time I arrived. When I texted her, she said she'd be down in just a minute. I was waiting in my car when she came down in a rush, swung open the passenger side door, and leaned over the seat. She started kissing me all over, and her hands were everywhere. I was wearing my shorts, so she had an easy time as she started feeling my cock, which had been hard since the first phone call. She started rubbing my cock over the shorts, and then she finally pulled it out.

She whispered in my ear saying that, "You have a huge cock," and then she went lower and started kissing my cock all over and finally sucking it deep in her mouth, sucking it like a lollypop. While I was enjoying her talents and moaning with joy, she went deeper and ended up licking my balls with my cock down her throat. I took a large grab at her ass, and was pleased to find that she was only wearing pajamas without any panties. My hand went even lower as I caressed her, and I started rubbing a finger on her asshole. She was closing and opening her butt hole when my finger was feeling it, which I assumed meant that she was enjoying it a lot.

Then she whispered in my ears, "Fuck me, please."

I lifted her legs high in the car, her pussy lips wide open, and I could literally see the juices dripping. I started licking her pussy, and after a moment I slid a digit into her tight butthole. She kept on saying, "Fuck me please."

Finally I inserted my cock in her pussy very slowly, as I knew she was most likely a virgin. While I was fucking her back and forth her pussy was making noises, wet noises. I kept on fucking her for 6 to 7 minutes. Then I told her go doggy style at the back seat of the car. She agreed , spreading her ass wide open as if she wanted it in her ass. I could clearly see her asshole closing and opening as I continued prodding into her tight vagina. Finally my cock was wet enough for her tight ass. I plunged my cock in her butthole without any further warning. She was moaning , then she said, "Fuck me harder!"

I rammed my cock as far down as it could go within her asshole. She yelped in a bit of pain, but began wracking her body as I rubbed on her clit and continued pounding away. As she had an earth shattering orgasm, I spilled my seed inside her virgin asshole and kept pounding until she begged me to stop.

Anal Sex for Two 70-Year-Old Ladies at the RV Park

It's always been interesting listening to other people talk about their relationships with their wives, girlfriends and so forth, but I always thought that it was far better to participate than to listen or read what was going on. My life and experiences took place all over the world when it came to women, and I thought I was more than proficient when it came to being intimate with a woman.

About two years ago I decided to buy an RV and tour the country. One of my stops took me to a little town in New Mexico that was devoted to senior citizens . . . but ones that were active. After about a week in my park, walking around and saying hello to all, I noticed how open and friendly folks were. My neighbors on both sides were attractive, well-kempt women in their late 70's who showered me with baked goods and dinner plates with wonderful items that I'd never be able to cook myself. Frankly, I thought I'd really landed in a wonderful place.

My two "ladies" were out in the shade during the day, and at night they'd be at one home or the other while their husbands were off for the evening at the local Casinos. One evening, Doris came to the door and asked if she could come in. I asked her in and as I was making coffee for us noticed that she wasn't shy about letting my see that she had nothing on under her dress. She had sat back in my captain's chair and allowed me a full and long look at the lovely bush that resided between her slim athletic legs.

When I offered her coffee, she made it a point to lean over excessively and allow me to see that her pert little breasts were not contained in a bra as one would expect from most women her age. She mentioned that she'd be more comfortable on the couch and as she got up, made it a point to rub her breasts against me in a most delicious and delightful manner. As she sat down she noticed a slight bulge in my pants and with a girlish giggle asked, "Are you a little excited?"

I told her that I was and that I hadn't been with a woman for a few months as I was travelling around the country in my newly acquired RV. She coyly brushed her hand against my pants where my cock was and said that it seemed I needed a little attention. I told her that her being married and her husband coming home in a bit might pose a problem. She told me that he usually stayed in town for the weekends when he went to the Casino, as he drank a bit and it was far safer that way.

She no sooner finished her sentence than her cell rang and her husband announced in a thick slurred voice that coming home would be out of the question tonight. I made a weak complaint about her being married, but she already had the zipper down in my trousers and was pulling my cock out and fondling it gently. As my cock grew she began to lick and tongue the tip of it and gently suck on just the head until I came to a full erection.

At that point I felt I was going to explode and she suddenly slapped the head of my cock. "Not so fast" she said softly. "I need a little work on my pussy, and I mean to get what I need." At that she slipped rapidly out of her skirt and relaxed on her back holding her pussy open with both hands and said ... "Suck my clit slowly and softly."

I was amazed at how sweet and succulent her cunt was. It wasn't old smelling or nasty as I thought an old broad's pussy would be. She moaned and groaned and moved around and then suddenly erupted and came in my mouth. I was surprised and just about to get up when I felt someone gently holding me in place. I turned to see Alice, my other "lady," standing above me completely naked and rubbing her pussy that was already glistening with come. I turned to Alice and she spread her legs around my face and gently lowered my head back on the couch and let me suck on her clit until she came all over my face. At this point, I was delirious but nothing had happened to my now gorged cock.

Doris was first and she bent me over to suck on my balls my Alice softly played with my cock. I started to say something about their husbands coming back and was quickly told to shut up and, "Go with the flow!"

It didn't take long for Alice to take my cock in her mouth, stand up and let Doris start tonguing her pussy. Meanwhile Doris gently repositioned herself and lowered her pussy over my mouth and let me tongue her again. Within minutes I came and not a drop came out of Alice's mouth. She kept sucking until I thought I was full of air and brought me to another erection.

The two ladies then repositioned so that one was sucking on ones cunt and the other had her ass in the air. I didn't know whose ass was up, but I heard Doris say fuck my ass. I slowly slid my cock in to her waiting ass and slowly fucked her until she started moaning and telling me that she loved ass fucking more than pussy fucking.

Meanwhile Alice was busy sucking on Doris's clit and getting her to come over and over while I built to a climax that ended with a rupture of come that started oozing out of Doris's asshole. As she slowly lowered herself to the floor, Alice starting licking the come out her ass and bending over in a position that only said . . . fuck me like that.

My cock was aching and I knew there wasn't another drop of come in me but the "ladies" kept moaning, kissing one another and me and begging for hard massaging of their tits, ass and pussy. I could feel the slippery wetness of come from both of them and the jism that I had put in Doris's ass and pussy, and the two of them just kept kissing and sucking on one another and myself. After a slow relaxing time laying together, I felt my cock begin to twitch and I ran my hand over Alice's ass and pussy and she simply rolled over, got up on her elbows and put her nicely turned ass into the air.

Doris licked Alice's asshole until it was nice and wet, jerked on my cock and got it slippery and then helped me slowly bury it all the way into Alice's hot little ass hole. She squeezed as I slowly buried it completely in her ass hole and then squeezed my cock as I slowly withdrew it until just the tip was left in. This went on for several wonderful moment s and then I buried it fully in her asshole and filled her with come, which immediately began to ooze out of her hole around my cock. Doris quickly got up under us to lick both of us clean.

On and on we went all night fucking and sucking in so many positions that I thought I'd pass out. In the morning as we fucked and sucked ourselves in to awareness I knew that many a night would come in the future for me to enjoy more of these lovely "ladies" and their penchant for anything kinky and rough.

Sucking Swittles Out of Her Butthole: An Erotica with Anal Candy Insertion and Anal Sex

Bite-Size Gabriella was a sizzling hot petite girl that worked at my dentist's office. My visits had become more frequent because of an obsession with candy taking its toll on my teeth. I don't know where she was from, but her exotic look suggested a Latin American persuasion. A perfect 5'4", 100 LB, thick little 22 year-old body, straight black hair and emerald green eyes. If Helen of Troy caused a war, this girl would cause a war of the worlds.

She was always friendly and smiled but I would never get a chance to talk to her much because it was a high volume practice. One day I saw her while I was jogging and started chatting with her. She had this sexy Spanish accent that would give anyone a bulge in the pants. After speaking a while, I talked her into going to dinner. I made sure to take her to Garibaldi's on 8th, one of the classiest restaurants in town. I had to impress the hell out of her right off the bat. No room for fuck-ups.

So we talked and had a sumptuous lobster dinner. I had the waiter bring us a bottle of Dauphin Noir that I knew would put us both in a good, relaxed mood. The whole time all I could think about is stuffing my 8" cock into this hottie. So I pay for dinner and give the waiter a generous tip, and we walk out laughing, hand in hand. We get in the car and out of nowhere, Gabriella leans over and kisses me and starts stroking my cock, which had been hard ever since I picked her up.

I'm kinda looking around to make sure no one creeps up on us, like some cop or something. I suddenly hear a zipping sound and then feel her thick Latin lips wrapping around my dick head. I was actually a bit shocked. I did not know she liked me THAT much. She just kept sucking on my cock while her tongue massaged my flesh. Holy fuck, this girl could suck! So I ask her if she wants to go to my house for a bit more privacy. Reluctantly, she took my cock out of her hungry mouth, and we drove off. The whole way she is rubbing her pussy and moaning, and I'm just hauling ass trying to get home without crashing or getting a ticket so I can just pound her tanned little ass.

When we got home, I ripped off her clothes and laid her on the bed and told her to just be still. She had a puzzled look on her face. I go in the drawer and pull out a bag of Swittles bite size candy, my favorite. I also pull out the watermelon flavored lubricant I had gotten in the mail a few days before. I just start slurping and her on her little clit while I finger fuck her anus with the lube. You have never seen a more gorgeous pussy than her waxed little cunt. I open the bag of Swittles and start stuffing her tight, creamy asshole with them slowly. She is just losing it.

After I made her cum hard, I started licking her asshole and begging for my candy back. So she's moaning as she squeezes the Swittles slowly into my mouth. Then I just started sucking the candy out and you could just see the juice just oozing out of her hot little twat. Now, I would SUCK a hot girl's asshole plain, but I'm a candy freak so it made it all the more sublime. By now her waxed little pussy is just pure cream and my thick, 8" cock is like portland concrete. I start fucking her tight little cunt and I can barely stuff my cock in there.

In the meantime, I unwrap a watermelon Sharms lollipop and start twirling it between her thick, juicy Latin lips. She is zombied out in ecstasy. I stop fucking her for a second so I can suck on her clit some more while I twirl the lollipop in and out of her tender, creamy little asshole. She's just jerking from the intense pleasure. She let out a shriek and a squirt of thick juice out of her pussy. All of a sudden she grabs my stiff cock and starts working it up her ass. I thought I was gonna die. I was actually kinda surprised I had actually gotten this far. Now, this is just insane. As I'm stuffing her tight asshole, I can see my dick is covered in blue, red and all the other Swittles colors. After a while, I sat up, leaned back, and started bouncing her hot Latin ass hard on my cock.

What a delicious little fuck! I felt the most spine-tingling sensation as I plunged my cock deeper inside her, and she was almost drooling from the intensity. After about 10 minutes though, I could barely hold my cum. She told me to pull out for a second to stop from ejaculating. Then she laid me back and started deep throating my dick nice and slow. I mean, I could actually feel it going down her throat. Her lips were covered in Swittles juice. It only took about 5 minutes for me to ejaculate in a most explosive way.

She jerked back a bit but just kept sucking and swallowing until I was so sensitive I had to beg her to stop. I never saw a drop of cum and trust me, it felt like I shot a gallon of semen. She rubbed my cock on her precious tanned face and kissed it a few times. I was literally on the verge of tears. In my 43 years, I have NEVER fucked a girl that was hotter, sexier, or more willing to do ANYTHING than Gabriella.

Afterwards, we both just plopped down and fell asleep. After about an hour I feel something on my cock and when I open my eyes, there she was deepthroating my thick cock again. In my head I'm like: "Holy fuck! Here we go again and I'm all out of Swittles, shit!"